VOLUME 2

Silly Nomads™

Go Ninja Crazy

By M. E. Mohalland and J. L. Lewis
Illustrated by Kate Santee

MOHALLAND LEWIS LLC

6573
ISBN 978-0-9897106-2-6

"That dog barks too loud. I know he's a dog, but why does he have to bark so much?"

"Shhh, don't move. Don't even breathe."

"*Uuuuuhhh.*" Naddih drew in a huge breath of air and clamped his hand over his mouth.

"What are you doing?"

"You said don't breathe."

"You should breathe. I meant don't talk."

"But I'm not talking, Suhcrom. *OUCH!* Don't pinch me."

Hamburg's mother looked around the yard one last time. "Humph," she sighed. "Shut your mouth, Sticky. You're giving me a headache."

BANG! The door slammed as Hamburg's mother turned out the light and darkness filled the yard once again. The boys looked at each other. No words were necessary. They bolted with lightning speed. Suhcrom took a flying leap, scraping his leg as he straddled the fence. He glanced back at the chicken coop.

"Shucks, I wanted my book back!"

"Suhcrom, Suhcrom," Naddih whispered.

"Come on, man. Let's get out of here!"

"I tryin', but my foot keeps sliding."

"Here, grab my hand. Use your feet to crawl up, but go light."

"Go light?"

"Yeh, don't use all your weight ... I said, 'Go light,' I don't want to fall off the fence."

G-r-r-r-r-r-r-r. ARRRF-ARRRF-ARRRF!

"Hurry, Naddih, before we get eaten alive!"

Suhcrom's hand stung as he gripped the rough, pebbly cinder blocks. He leaned over as far as he dare and pulled his brother up to the top. Together, they jumped into Mikal's yard. Before they knew it, they were up and over the next fence into their own yard. Back to safety, they paused to catch their breath — and then burst into nervous laughter. Suhcrom wiped the sweat from his forehead. *Hiccup-hiccup.*

"Holy Moly! That was close," Naddih panted. "We could've been caught."

"Yeh, or worse, mauled to death by Sticky Fingers!" *Hiccup-hiccup.*

"We didn't finish the mission, Suhcrom."

"I know ... I want my book."

"So what book is it?"

"Nah, don't worry about it. I'll tell you later."

They skipped into their house, laughing and shoving each other, having made curfew with only seconds to spare. They halted when they saw Enomih, their older sister, sitting on the couch studying. She looked up at them and glared suspiciously.

"Where have you two been? And what's so funny?"

"Nuttin' you need to know about," said Suhcrom.

"Look at her, studying again." Naddih tapped his brother on the arm and tipped his nose in the air. "Study all you want. *When mi get bigga, mi a go show yu who is smaata.*"

The boys ran off to their room to get ready for bed. *HICCUP! HICCUP!*

"You want some sugar water, Suhcrom?"

"Sugar water? No, I want my book!"

"What's going on? You only hiccup when you're nervous ... or done something bad."

"I lent Hamburg the book, that's what I did."

"Which book?"

"The book Jomfeh bought for Enomih to study for the Common Entrance Exam."

"What book is that? Come on, man, spill the ketchup!"

"You mean spill the beans. You don't need to know everything, but I'll tell you this much. It starts with 'the' and ends with 'English.'"

"What?"

"*The New First Aid in English.*"

"Are you crazy? You gave away Enomih's book? Jomfeh's going to be really mad."

"I didn't give it away. I just let him borrow it, but I

need it to study. You've got to help me get it back, little brother. You've got to help me."

"Okay, I will help you. Up, up and away!"

"Man, that's Superman. We're ninjas, remember? And this mission is really important. So listen, Naddih, I have an idea. Let's set up an obstacle course in the back yard."

"Set up an obstacle course?"

"Yes, that's how the real ninjas train."

"What does that have to do with your book?"

"If we're going to get this book back, we need to build up our strength and endurance."

"Oh yes, yes, strength and *imboorance*. What exactly is *imboorance?*"

"Endurance, Naddih, not *imboorance*. Endurance is when you do something for a long time, like for an eternity, but you don't get tired. 'Tired' is the enemy. We must defeat it."

Suhcrom held up his arm, flexed his biceps and strutted proudly back and forth.

"See my muscles? They're big, and gigantic... and really strong. 'Tired' is afraid of these. *Jus imagine when mi get dem bigga!*"

Naddih gave Suhcrom's biceps a squeeze and then flexed his own muscles. He frowned. "Wow, I need some Popeye spinach."

"You'll need three cans of spinach every day to help those muscles!"

"So how are we going get *imboorance*?"

"We're going to lift weights."

"And should we drink some of that magic potion, too, like those guys on TV? You know, the ones with those huge muscles in their arms and legs, and their chest? *Mi tink dem hav muscle inna dem eye lash, too.*"

"No, man, no. Never, *EVER* drink that stuff. That will make your brain shrink... like *gungo peas.* Then you won't remember the important things like your name, where you live, and how to tie your own shoe-lace... and you'll be wanderin' around Jamaica talkin' to yourself about all kinds of nonsense."

"*Imboorance* training sounds hard," Naddih said as he hopped into bed. "I better get some rest."

Suhcrom heard the wind howling as he turned off the light. He peered at the window and watched as the coconut tree branches swayed to and fro in the dim moonlight. Suddenly, there was a big crash. *BAM!*

"What was that?"

"I think it's Mr. Broomie," Suhcrom whimpered.

"*MR. BROOMIE!*" Naddih clutched his pillow to his chest.

Suhcrom bolted upright. His jaw dropped as he

stared at the monstrous shadow darting back and forth. It lunged across the wall, surrounding them in darkness.

"It's him! It's him!"

"*A-A-A-A-A-A-A-A-H!!!*" they both screamed and quickly hid under their covers.

CHAPTER 2

Annoying Rooster

It was early morning in Portsmouth, Jamaica. The gusty wind filled the air with the familiar smell of fishy sea water. Naddih was still asleep, but Suhcrom had been lying awake for what seemed like hours — all because of the annoying rooster next door.

Cock-a doodley-do! Cock-a doodley-do!

"Oh no, not today, man, not today," he groaned. "I'm tired, and it's still dark outside. I swear you do this just to make me mad! Every morning you do the same thing — hop on the fence, face my window, and start hollerin' at me."

Cock-a doodley-do!

"Shut up you good-for-nothing rooster!"

Cock-a doodley-do!

"That's it. I can't take this anymore!" Suhcrom jumped out of bed. He ran outside in nothing but his tightey-whiteys and hurled a rock. "Take that, you stupid rooster!"

BANG! The rock slammed against the zinc roof of Mr. Broomie's shed and bounced several times before landing on the ground. *Bing, bong . . . Ker-plunk!*

Mr. Broomie ran outside, yelling wildly.

"What's going on out here? Who's throwing things at my shed?"

Suhcrom shuddered at the sound of Mr. Broomie's voice. He was thankful he couldn't see him over the fence. In fact, for the entire five years he and Naddih had lived in the neighborhood of Palmerston Close with their sister, Enomih, and their father, whom they affectionately called "Jomfeh," they had never had a glimpse of Mr. Broomie—not even once. The only thing they'd ever heard were stories about him flying around at night, smashing his broom bristles against the windows, scaring all the kids half to death!

Suhcrom hightailed back into the house before Mr. Broomie could utter another word. He scurried into the bedroom just as Naddih was getting up.

"A weh yu deh outside inna yu underpants fa?"

"That crazy rooster..." Suhcrom sputtered. "I think my blood pressure is high now."

"Blood pressure? You're just ten years old... and I'm eight. Only old people, like Miss Velma, worry about blood pressure."

"That rooster is annoying! *Aargh*, forget about him. You ready to do some training?"

The boys quickly dressed and raced to the kitchen

where their father was making breakfast. The aroma of fried eggs and dumplin' made them hungry!

"Good morning, my sons. What are you two doing today?"

"Watching cartoons," Suhcrom grinned. He grabbed an egg and a few dumplings, went into the living room, and turned on the TV. It was tuned into the annual telethon from one of the international Christian organizations. Every year, one of the pastors stood before the audience, pleading for money to provide food, water, clothing and education for the children in Ethiopia.

"Oh man, they're asking for money again? Where are my cartoons?" He changed the channel and settled into his favorite position on the couch. "Hey Naddih, *He-Man* is coming on."

"Oh, cool. *He-Man and the Masters of the Universe!*" Naddih ran in from the kitchen and plopped himself on the floor directly in front of the TV.

Move, man, move! You're blocking my view."

Naddih didn't pay any attention. He lay in a trance, starring glassy-eyed into the screen and didn't budge.

Suhcrom stomped across the room, pulled his brother by the legs and dragged him back away from the TV. "I said *MOOOVE!*"

He flopped on the couch, eager to enjoy the cartoons, but quickly grew restless. He couldn't stop thinking about the Ethiopian children. *I do care about them, Lord, I do. But I love cartoons! I promise, when I save a whole dollar, I'll send it to Ethiopia. I promise.*

"So what you want to do now?" asked Naddih. "Cartoons are over."

"Yeh, and I missed half of them. Okay, let's build our obstacle course."

"Won't Jomfeh wonder what we're doing back there?"

"He went to the market."

"What about Enomih?"

"Don't worry. If she bothers us, we'll just tell her we're doing chores. Come on, we've got a lot to do."

The boys rushed outside. The ground was still a little muddy from an overnight thunderstorm, and as they scampered about the yard, the warm pasty earth oozed up between their toes, splattering their ankles.

"Man, this reminds me of the cow pen."

Naddih giggled. "You mean like in those stories Jomfeh always told us about wakin' up in the morning with cow pooh all over the yard?"

"Yeh, man, that stuff was stinky!"

"Is that true? Was there really cow pooh all over the yard?"

"Yes, when we lived in that little hut Mama rented for us."

"I don't remember that."

"You wouldn't. You were just a little baby without any teeth. This house is like a castle compared to that."

"Suhcrom, can we ask Sterlin and Rodney to come over? They'll want to be ninjas, too. If we were all ninjas, we could...."

"No, I told you before, we can't tell them. We can't tell anyone. If those guys find out, they'll make fun of us. And you can't tell them about our mission, either."

"But they're our best friends."

"No, man, I mean it. Nobody can know. Not Rodney, not Mikal, not Amos, and especially not Sterlin. He already told me I'm too old to be playing childish games. If they find out, they'll laugh their heads off!"

"What about Shanise? She won't tell anybody. She hardly talks."

"Then what's the use in telling her?"

"So I can get it off my chest."

"Why would you need to do that?"

"Because that's what old people do. I heard Jomfeh telling Miss Beverly that he needed to get some things off his chest."

"All right, all right, tell her if you want. Her mother

never lets her out to play anyway. But nobody else, you swear?"

"No man, no. I won't tell anybody else."

"Pinky swear?" Suhcrom extended his pinky and they hooked fingers to pledge their silence. "Okay, let's get our training course set up."

"Are we going to do all that stuff they showed on *American Ninja?*"

"Yes, we're going to lift weights, and do chin-ups and jumping jacks, and climb, too."

"*How wi a go do alla dat in one day?*" Naddih followed Suhcrom back into the house and straight to the kitchen closet. "What are you looking for?"

"A bar, or some kind of a handle," he said. He grabbed the broom. *Crack ... crack. SNAP!*

"What are you doing? Isn't that the new broom?"

"Don't worry, man. This is the old one. We've had it for two weeks!" Suhcrom tossed the bristles aside and continued to rummage through the closet. "Hmmm...."

"Now what are you looking for?"

"Something we can use for weights. Hey, look Naddih, empty paint cans."

"Empty paint cans? How do we make weights out of them, fill them with cement?"

"No, man, that would take days! We'll fill them with

water and hang them over the broom stick. Ha-ha, we'll
have our own set of barbells!"

"That's a great idea, just like Jackie Chan—only
he trains with big glass bottles of water. *Di paint cans
betta because dem no break!*"

"Yeh, just wait, Naddih, you'll see. Our muscles will
get huge! We'll be strong from our fingers to our toes!
And we'll have '*imboorance*' too," he teased.

Eager to test the weights out right away, Suhcrom
carried the cans and broomstick outside. Naddih helped
by spreading out some cinder blocks to make a platform.

"Hold on, Suhcrom, I'll be right back."

"Where are you running off to?"

Naddih raced into the house. When he returned, his
hands were cupped, full of water, and his cheeks were
stretched out as big as a balloon. A stream of water
dribbled down his chin. He giggled as he spit the water
into one of the cans.

"*Wi need waata inna di cans.*"

"Just get the hose, man. It's right there." Suhcrom
grabbed the garden hose and turned on the water. He
filled the cans up, up, up … all the way to the brim.

"That's a *LOT* of water, Suhcrom."

"Get the broomstick, Naddih. Slide it through the
handles."

The boys stood back and smiled at each other, admiring their invention.

"Okay, the training starts now. Go ahead, Naddih. You go first. See how long you can hold these weights. I'll start counting."

"Wait, Suhcrom, wait. You don't have to use your mouth to count."

Naddih reached into his pocket and pulled out a sock. From the sock, he pulled a crumpled wad of paper. Suhcrom watched intently as Naddih peeled off several layers of newspaper, and then layer after layer of toilet paper. His eyes lit up when Naddih held out his hand.

"Where did you get that?"

"I found it. Right here in the yard. *Mi did a preten fi be a pirate anna dig fi treasure!*"

They gazed at the watch in Naddih's hand. It was the most valuable thing either of them had ever found. It had a bright yellow band, and on the face was the Superman emblem.

"It wasn't working, so I took the battery out of the old Mickey Mouse watch. That one worked, but it didn't have any straps."

"Wow, this is amazing. It even has a second hand." Suhcrom slipped the watch around his wrist. "We're good now! Go ahead, Naddih. Pick up the cans. Ready, set, go… I said go, man, go!"

Naddih stared at the weights. He braced his feet and drew in a deep breath. With legs bent, he pulled on the bar with all of his might. It barely moved.

"Holy Macaroni, Suhcrom, these weigh a million pounds! How can I get bigger muscles if I can't lift the weights? *Mi need Mista Swazenaada to help mi wid dis.*"

"*Swazenaada?* Don't you mean Mista Shaz… I mean Mista Shorz… never mind, the guy with the big stuffed pillows in his biceps? Okay, okay, I'll just take some water out."

"*Mi like dat betta.*"

"And here's my new rule—a five-second penalty if any water spills out… even one little tiny drop."

"That's not fair."

"It's the same thing Jackie Chan's master did to punish him for messing up in training. So stop your bawlin,' man. Ninjas don't complain."

"*Mi na bawl, mi jus a speak mi mind.*"

"Okay, done. I took some water out. Now it's my turn to try. Time me."

"Oh, so now Mr. Big Muscle wants to go first."

"Come on, time me."

"Okay, go! One, two, three ...." Naddih counted out loud as the second hand ticked. "... Twenty-nine, thirty, thirty-one ... thirty ...."

"*Aargh.*" Suhcrom grunted as he awkwardly lowered the weights to the ground.

"Holy Moly, thirty-one point five nine seven seconds, but we'll call it thirty-two!"

"Thirty-two seconds? That's a record! Okay, now you do it." Suhcrom took the watch and gave Naddih the signal to begin. "Start NOW!"

"Wait, start at twenty."

"Yeh right, twenty my big toe! You will be lucky if you make it to ten!"

BONG! SPLASH! The cans slipped from Naddih's grip. They crashed on the ground and toppled over, spilling water all across the cinder blocks.

"How many seconds was that?"

"I was just about to start counting."

"That's good enough for today. I'm tired. My muscles hurt—and they're still sagging!"

"Your pants are sagging, too."

"*Mi dun, man. Mi wi wok pon mi imboorance lataron.*"

"Hey, what about all this spilled water? That's a five-second penalty."

Naddih shrugged his shoulders. "Penalty yourself." He hooked a finger through his belt loop and gave his pants a tug as he walked away.

"Don't forget about our mission," Suhcrom called out.

CHAPTER 3

Soccer Some Books

"**S**uhcrom, you want to arm wrestle?"

"Not with those dirty hands."

Naddih licked his fingers and wiped them on his shirt. "How 'bout now?"

"I'd beat you in a second."

Their father chuckled to himself, overhearing the conversation as he entered the kitchen. He set down a bag of food from the market, and began to wash some dishes.

"*A wah yuh boys a talk 'bout?*"

"Nothing," replied Suhcrom.

"We're training," Naddih said.

"Training? What kind of training?"

"Umm … soccer," said Suhcrom, punching his brother's arm.

"Soccer training, huh? All this playing—but no studying! Why don't you two go soccer some books? Read, read, read. I keep telling you how important reading is." He shook his head and waved the boys away.

Naddih chuckled. "Sometimes Jomfeh don't make sense, you know. How are we going to soccer books? Or play with books? Oh, oh wait, his favorite—dance with books?"

"Come on, Naddih, let's get out of here before Jomfeh asks us to wash books!"

The boys scampered back outside. Suhcrom gave Naddih a nudge, motioning for him to grab some cinder blocks.

"Let's make a ramp so we can practice our jumps."

"Cool. I like jumping. It's a lot easier than lifting those heavy paint cans!"

"Now remember, ninjas don't make any sound when they jump. Nobody can hear us when we jump into Hamburg's yard. Nobody."

"Did you forget about Sticky? He hears everything, even when we breathe."

"No man, we'll be so quiet, even Sticky won't hear us."

The boys stacked several cinder blocks and propped a sturdy board against them. Suhcrom was the first to test it. He dug his toes into the dirt and then charged up the ramp. He jumped high in the air, gave his heels a click, and landed softly on the balls of his feet.

"Wow!" he screeched. "This is fun!"

"Let me try it, Suhcrom."

"One … two … three … four …." Naddih counted out ten paces from the ramp. Slowly, he rocked his body back and forth, and then licked his finger.

"What are you waiting for?"

"Hold on, hold on. Don't rush me! I'm checking the direction of the wind."

"Man, don't be so silly. Just jump—or I'll impose a penalty for taking too long!"

Naddih made a mad dash. He sprinted at the speed of light and bounded up the ramp, flying high in the air.

"Woohoo, yippee, ha-ha!" he bellowed. He sailed through the air, screaming with delight, certain his jump was higher than Suhcrom's. He dashed around the yard, spinning in circles, dancing his favorite Jamaican *ska* moves. He stood in front of Suhcrom and took a bow.

"What did you think? Pretty good, huh?"

"Yes, yes, Naddih. It was great... but you screamed. We're ninjas, remember? Ninjas don't make noise."

"You screamed, too."

"Not 'til I was done."

"What difference does that make?"

"Try it again. But this time no noise."

Naddih went back to his starting position and repeated his jump, landing as softly as he could. He smiled at Suhcrom, waiting for his approval.

"No man, no. You came down hard on your heels. Do it again until you get it right." Suhcrom chuckled while

Naddih did another jump. "No, no, no," he giggled. "I'm trying to help you, man. One more time ... and no noise!"

"I didn't make any noise."

"Yes you did."

"You're hearing things. My big toe didn't even touch the ground. *Because di big toe wud mek di most noise.*"

Suhcrom smirked. "It has to be perfect."

"I need a break. Do we have any juice? Mi so *blahdy tirsty.*"

"Ha-ha-ha, are you trying to speak like that British man again?"

Naddih vanished into the house. When he returned, he was carrying two glasses of lemonade. He took a big sip from one of the glasses and handed it to Suhcrom.

"Did you just lick my cup?"

"No, man, I just took a tiny sip."

"Yeh, but your mouth touched it. Why didn't you take a sip from your own cup?"

Naddih took a big gulp from the other glass. "Oh, okay. Do you want this one, then?"

"Not now!"

"Hey, Suhcrom, do you think we are ready for our mission?"

"*Yah mon*, we'll be ready—as soon as you learn how to control your big toe!"

CHAPTER 4

Ninja Stars

lang! Clunk! SLAM! Naddih hunted around the living room, pulling things out of the cupboards, looking in drawers, and even checking under the couch cushions.

"You know what we need, Suhcrom? Ninja darts."

"Ninja darts?"

"Yeh, those shiny metal things that the ninjas throw at their enemies."

"Oh, you mean stars?"

"Yes, and a *boombalang.*"

"I don't know 'bout no boomerang. The last one I threw never came back. I couldn't believe that stupid thing. I mean, I threw it the same way Indiana Jones did in... what was that movie? Wasn't it *Raiders of the Lost Ark?* I don't remember. Anyway, instead of knocking down the bottles and cans and coming back, it missed the cans and went straight through the glass of Mr. Simon's old car. No ice cream money for eight months—eight months, man. Might as well have sent me to jail! Depriving a child of ice cream is despicable."

"Despicable?"

"Yes, despicable."

"What does that mean?"

"I don't know, Sylvester always says it to Tweety Bird. Anyway, it's sad."

"Oh...."

"It sure would be nice to have those stars, though."

"So what do we have around here that we can we use?"

"Let me think." Suhcrom scratched his head and rested his chin in his hand. His eyes lit up as a huge smile spread across his face. "Why don't we make one?"

"How wi a go mek a star outta metal?"

"Not metal, Naddih, wood. There's a ton of it out back. We'll make one out of wood."

"Just one? You mean we have to share? I want my own."

"We'll start with one. If it works, we can always make more."

Naddih followed Suhcrom out to the wood pile, and while his brother searched through the scrap boards, he did some exploring of his own. An interesting piece of wood caught his eye.

"Hey, Suhcrom, watch this." *SNAP! "Mi stronga now!"*

"Stronger? That's just a stick."

"A stick is like a board."

"No man, that's just a skinny little stick. Anybody could have broken that. Even our buddy, Mouse. You need muscles like these to break a board. See, Naddih? This is what you want right here." He bobbed his head from side to side in boyish arrogance and kissed his bulging biceps. "Ha! Your muscles still look like Popeye, the Sailor Man—when he's not eating his spinach!"

"They do not. You tease me all the time. Forget about my muscles. Let's make our ninja star. Did you find a piece of wood yet?"

"Yes, I've got one right here. Now we need some tools. I'm going to see what I can find in Jomfeh's toolbox."

"Suhcrom, you know he doesn't want us in there—not without his permission."

"Mi know, mi know."

"He'll be really mad if he finds out."

"Yeh, you're right."

"We're lucky he never found out we took his knife on our nomad adventure."

"We need something really sharp...something we can carve with. Let me look around. I'll be right back."

Suhcrom went into the house and searched through all the drawers, but there was nothing. He reached for his father's toolbox, and then hesitated. *There's got to be something around here that we can use.* He searched some more, and finally, several minutes later, went back outside, smiling proudly.

"I found something—this knife on these nail clippers!"

The boys each took turns, carefully carving the wood the best they could. Before long, Naddih slumped on the ground and gently rubbed his hands.

"Suhcrom, we've been working on this for hours. I need a break. My *ataritis* is coming on."

"Arthritis? Only old people, who are like ninety or a hundred years old, have that. You're just a kid, a baby chickling. Give me that. I'll work on it for a while."

"Hey! I didn't say I wanted to quit. I just need a little break... like ten seconds. One... two... three... four.... I'm ready again."

"Too late. I've got it now. I'll finish it."

Naddih's frustration turned to curiosity as he watched his brother work. Suhcrom went at that thing like a man on a mission to find gold in the desert. He carved and carved; then he filed, and carved again. After what seemed to be forever, he had etched a star out of the wood and had smoothed off the edges as much as he possibly could.

"Mi dun wid dis ting ya."

"No, Suhcrom, it needs to be smoother."

"Look man, we've been working on this for hours. I'm tired. And my fingers are burning. Here, you can work on it some more if you want."

"No, it's okay. My *ataritis* will be worse if I work on it any longer, but let's color it."

Naddih ran into the house. He grabbed his box of crayons from the side pocket of the couch, where he stored most of his prized possessions, and quickly returned. He pulled out the black crayon and carefully colored every inch of wood.

"There, how does that look, Suhcrom?"

"Let me see that. Give it to me. Let me put the finishing touch on it."

"Finishing touch? It's already finished. "

"Come on, man. Let me see it."

"Look at it from there." Naddih held the star close to his chest, protecting it in his hands.

"Holy Smackaroni! It looks really good."

"It should. It took us like twenty hours to make it!"

"Let's test it out."

"Who's going to throw first?" asked Naddih. "Maybe the littlest brother should go first."

"Why should you get to throw it first?"

"Ok, pick a number from one to a thousand."

"What?"

"Just pick one."

"Okay, one thousand."

"No. I was thinking of nine hundred ninety nine and a half."

"Okay Mista Smarty Pants, you go first."

"Wait, Suhcrom, why don't we throw it at a board with one of those bully eyes on it?"

"Okay, but we'll have to get a big board—and make a really huge bull's eye, because the last time you drew it, we needed a magnifying glass to see it!"

Whoosh ... "Oh, I missed."

Whoosh ... "Ooooh, I got inside the circle!"

Whoosh..."Oh, I missed again! *Aargh*, how many times have you hit the bull's eye, Suhcrom?"

"Zero. How many times have you hit it?"

"Naught."

"Not?"

"Naught. I learned that word in class the other day."

"You should have learned that word in kindergarten."

"Listen, Suhcrom. The word is 'naught.' N-a-u-...."

"Oh, I get it ... g-h-t. Why couldn't you just say 'zero'?"

They were just about to call it quits when Naddih spotted a bird perched on the edge of Mr. Broomie's roof.

He glanced at Suhcrom. He thought about asking if he could throw the star at the bird because he believed in the democratic process. But he didn't ask this time. The star was in his hot little hand and he was itching to throw it... and throw it he did! A gust of wind caught it as it sailed through the air, whipping it around and around and around. And, instead of hitting the bird, the star landed right in the middle of Mr. Broomie's roof. Naddih winced.

"Uh-oh."

"*A weh yu do dat fa?*" Suhcrom yelled. He threw his arms up in the air. "I can't believe this... after working for hours, Naddih, hours! Now our star's up there on Mr. Broomie's roof, of all places." He flopped on the ground and buried his head in his hands.

"I'm sorry, Suhcrom. I was trying to hit that bird. I even closed one of my eyes to get the bird in my sight — just like you taught me." He raised his hand and extended his pinky.

"Your eyes must be crooked! And don't point that pinky finger at me."

"Come on, man. Have some mercy on me!"

"There's no way we're *EVER* going to get it back now."

"Maybe we could ask Mr. Broomie to get it for us."

"Ask Mr. Broomie? No way!"

"Miss Velma is right next door. Maybe she could ask him. She's not afraid of anybody!"

"No man, no."

"What about Jomfeh?"

"Are you kidding me? We can't ask him. We would have to tell him what we were doing—and that would blow our cover. We wouldn't be able to finish our mission. No, just forget it. It's on Mr. Broomie's roof, and that's where it's going to stay."

Suhcrom shook his head. His shoulders slumped as he headed towards the house. He was just about to open the door when something caught his attention—something out of the corner of his eye. He paused.

"Hey Naddih, come here. Look...."

"What is it?"

Suhcrom's face lit up like he'd just won the Jamaican lottery. "Wow, we just hit the jackpot. Hurry, help me take the screen out of this window."

"Are you sure we should do this? We need that screen to keep the mosquitos out. Those mosquitos suck our blood at night."

"It's okay, Naddih. It'll be fine. It's falling apart anyway. Jomfeh and Enomih will never notice. Just remember, don't open the window at night. I repeat, don't open the window!"

"You mean not even a little? Not even to let some cool sea breeze in? What if it gets hot?"

"No, no, mi seh no, man."

After dismantling the screen, they ended up with four small pieces of metal... four shiny silver "ninja stars," plus two longer pieces they could use as swords. The boys couldn't believe their fortune.

"What a stroke of luck!" exclaimed Suhcrom.

Naddih picked up one of the stars and held it high, admiring its beauty. As he gazed, the sunlight caught the tip of the star, creating a brilliant glow.

"Whoa!" They jumped back and gasped in disbelief.

"Suhcrom, it's happening again!"

Naddih stared at the gleaming star. He felt his hand quiver. The current pulsated through his whole body—just like the day in their nomad desert.

"Every ting betta now." Naddih sighed with relief. *"Every ting much betta."*

They giggled as they gathered their stars and swords and raced into the house to hide their new treasures. They couldn't wait to use them for their secret mission!

CHAPTER 5

Pop Quiz

"**S**uhcrom, Suhcrom."

"Yes Naddih?"

"Suhcrom."

"Yes Naddih, what is it? I answered you the first time. What do you want?"

"What about our big mission? Now that we have our stars and swords, it's time to do it like *REAL* ninjas."

"You're right. It's time to get my book back. We'll go just as soon as cartoons are done."

"We should go now, Suhcrom, while Enomih is studying… and before Jomfeh gets home."

Click. Click-click. Rattle-rattle-rattle. Bang! Bang! Bang!

"Suhcrom, Naddih, Enomih! Open this door. What have I told you about using the dead bolt?"

Suhcrom looked wide-eyed at Naddih. "Oh, no!"

"Should we make a dash for it?" Naddih whispered. "Uh-oh, too late."

"Quick Naddih, go open the door."

"No, you go. Why do I have to go all the time?"

"Go! Don't make him more mad."

Naddih went to the door, smiling sweetly at his father as he opened it.

"What have I told you about not using the deadbolt before six o'clock? Get a piece of paper—pop quiz."

"O-o-o-o-o-h," Naddih moaned.

"Turn that TV off. And where's Enomih? Naddih, go get your sister."

"Darn it, just when I really need my book it's not here," Suhcrom murmured. He searched for a pen and a pad of paper.

"Where are those kids? Enomih, come in here, and bring your brother."

Enomih came into the living room and gave her father a hug. She saw the bewildered look on Suhcrom's face.

"What's going on?"

"Pop quiz, that's what," grumbled Suhcrom.

"Where's your brother?" Jomfeh asked.

"I don't know. I thought he was in here watching cartoons with Suhcrom."

"He was supposed to go and get you... Naddih, Naddih! Come in here."

Suhcrom started towards the doorway. "I'll get him."

"Boy, just sit down and stay where you are."

Naddih peeked sheepishly around the doorway. He crept slowly into the room, whispering to Suhcrom as he passed by.

"I told you we should have left."

Enomih sat in the chair, waiting patiently. She crossed her ankles and placed her notebook neatly on her lap. With lips pursed, she grinned smugly at both of her brothers.

"I've been studying, Jomfeh. I'm ready," she gloated.

"Okay, I'm giving you twenty spelling words tonight," their father stated. "The first word is 'documentary.'"

Naddih's eyes lit up. "Jomfeh, did you say *doctamentry*?"

"What? Boy, what are you talking about? I said 'documentary.'"

"Can... can you repeat that?"

"Doc-u-mentary."

"Can you use it in a sentence?"

Jomfeh laughed softly and cleared his throat. "Okay. 'The documentary was a film about the magical land of Egypt.'"

"Oh, wait, wait. Can you repeat that again... please?"

"Boy, stop your nonsense! Just write the word."

Naddih leaned toward his sister. She quickly covered her paper.

"Stop cheating!"

"Man, we should have left for our mission," he mumbled.

"I'm so mad at Hamburg right now. I need my book!" Suhcrom sputtered under his breath. Beads of sweat dripped down his face, and his palms were so slippery he dropped his pen. *Hiccup! Hiccup!!* A grin of embarrassment spread slowly across his face when Naddih and Enomih giggled.

"Okay, the second word is 'telephone,'" their father announced.

"Wait, I'm still on my first word ... okay ... done," said Naddih.

Suhcrom sounded the word out loud as he wrote it down. "TEL-LEE-FONE."

"Is that two l's or one?" Naddih asked.

Enomih burst out laughing. "Man, what is wrong with you?"

"Boy, just spell the word."

Naddih wiggled in his seat. He scribbled some letters on his paper, and then crossed them out. He glanced at Suhcrom and gave his head a nod, searching for some kind of signal.

"Okay, the next word is ...."

The test proceeded slowly, word by word, until all twenty of the vocabulary words had been completed.

"Give me your papers," their father said calmly.

Enomih jumped up. She grinned as she handed her paper to her father, feeling certain she had a perfect score. Suhcrom shuffled across the room. He handed his damp paper to his father and grunted. His father raised his brow, but didn't say a word. Naddih was last. He scribbled a few more letters here and there, hoping it would be enough to pass. When he handed in his paper, his father looked at him sternly. He glanced at what Naddih had written.

"I tell you read, read, read. This is why you do poorly on your tests. Look at this, Naddih. Twenty points. And Suhcrom, you did not pass, either. Only sixty points."

"What did Enomih get?" Naddih asked with curiosity.

"As if we don't know," Suhcrom moaned.

"Go to your room now. Read your books. Read and study."

The boys grumbled as they shuffled out of the living room.

"I'm embarrassed of myself, and of you too, Suhcrom. How could we do so badly on that quiz?"

"Embarrassed of me? Don't be embarrassed of me. Be embarrassed of yourself. At least I got sixty. You only got twenty!"

"Mi dun wid studyin' for tonight."

"And the next time you say '*doctamentry*,' I'm going to make you give me ten dollars out of that ninety dollars you've saved up to buy your pigeon, that's wrapped in newspaper and stuffed in a sock... and hidden underneath all those clothes in the bottom of the barrel!"

"How you know 'bout that?" Naddih squinted and grabbed at Suhcrom's pockets.

"Who do you think you are, the police? Get your hands out of my pockets. I'm no thief, man." He shut the bedroom door behind them and they both flopped on their beds.

"Suhcrom, what about our mission? When are we going to finish it? Suhcrom...?"

Zzzzzzzzzz... zzzzzzzzzz... *snort*...

Naddih leaned over and flicked his brother's ear. "Suhcrom!"

"Ouch!"

"Wake up, man. Wake up. You sleep too much."

"What'd you do that for? I was just having a really good dream about out-spelling Enomih and Davina."

"That's impossible, Suhcrom. How would we ever be able to out spell Enomih? And who's Davina?"

"She's the smartest one in my class. She is really smart, like one of the smartest people I know. But she thinks she can out spell me!"

"Well, if she's the smartest one in your class, of course she can out spell you!"

"No man, no, not if I study my book. That's why I need it back."

"What's so great about this book?"

"What? You don't know what this book is? It has vocabulary and spelling and all kinds of important information about the English language. It's the one Jomfeh bought for Enomih to study for the Common Entrance Exam this year, and I need it to study for next year.

"You mean the one that has magical powers, and all you have to do is stare at the pages and the words just jump into your head?"

"Mi no know 'bout dat. All I know is that I lent it to Hamburg a while ago and he hasn't given it back. It must be working, though. Hamburg is out spellin' everyone... and you know that boy can't spell."

"He can't read, either," Naddih chuckled.

"One day I asked him to spell 'chicken' and he spelled 'kitchen.'"

"Maybe his hearing is bad, too!"

"The boy must've been thinking about food again. He knows I need it to study for my Common Entrance Exam. I overheard him on the bus the other day telling Amos he was going to ambush it!"

"Ambush?"

"Yeh, keep it for the rest of the year."

"But it's yours. So why don't you just ask him for it, Suhcrom?"

"No man, that's the point. Beat him at his own game. Sometimes you give me a headache with all your questions."

"Well, Jomfeh seh mi curious. Dats why mi ask so many questions."

"We need that book. If we could get it back, we could both out spell Enomih, and I could beat Davina and be first in the class in spelling. *Mi smaat, right?"*

"Suhcrom, why don't we get the book, and … and then dress up Sticky Fingers to play a joke on Hamburg? He's always playing jokes on us."

"That would be really funny, Naddih! I can't wait to see Hamburg's face when he realizes the book is gone and his stinky-mouthed dog is dressed in his favorite soccer jersey!"

CHAPTER 6

Desperate Measures

"Suhcrom," Naddih whispered, "Are you asleep yet?"

"Was I snoring?"

"Yes."

"So, a weh yu tink?"

"I have a *stimlacating* idea!"

"Stimlacating? What's so *'stimlacating'* about your idea?"

"It's something dangerous, but *REALLY* thrilling."

"Tell mi wa deh pon yu mind."

Naddih motioned for Suhcrom to move over. He jumped in the bed, grabbed a pillow and nestled in close to his brother.

"I was thinking about a different way we could get into Hamburg's yard...a surprise attack. We could dress like real ninjas, go up on the roof, hunt for enemy intruders between here and Hamburg's... and slay them with our ninja stars, or... or push them off the edge of the roof with our swords. We'll be heroes... and then we can get your...."

"Whoa, Naddih, wait a minute—go on the roof? How do we get to Hamburg's if we're on the roof?

"We jump across... from one roof to the next."

"Are you crazy man? That's three roofs—ours, Mikal's and then Hamburg's. "

"I told you it was *stimlacating.*

"The word is 'stimulating.' And that's not stimulating, it's dangerous."

"We'll destroy all the enemies, then jump down into Hamburg's yard and get your book."

"I would do just about anything to get my book back, but not this. It's not safe. And you? You're afraid of the dark. You think you're going to jump a roof at night?"

"Mi no fraid no more. Mi wi slay Mista Daakness. "

"Yeh, with your sword in one hand and my shirt tail in the other! Maybe I should knight you."

"Knight me? Really? Knight me then."

"Knights are smart. They're brave, and they protect the kingdom... and most of all they don't say *fool-fool* things."

Naddih leaped off the bed. "Okay, let's knight each other. Come on, Suhcrom, come on. I'll knight you, and you knight me." He grabbed his sword and rested it on Suhcrom's head. "Ommm... ommm." He waved it across

Suhcrom's right shoulder, then his left, and back to his head.

"Get on with it, man."

"I, Naddih, knight thee, Suhcrom, protector of our kingdom and universe, and everything within."

Suhcrom bowed, took the sword, and tapped it on Naddih's head. *Clunk. "Mi dun now.* Remember, Naddih, knights are smart and brave. They're not *fraidy-fraidy.*"

"Mi know, Suhcrom. Mi a go kill alla di enemies wid mi sword."

****

The next evening, after dark, the boys dressed in their makeshift ninja outfits. They snatched a couple of their father's old ties to use for belts. Grabbing their stars and swords, they slipped quietly out the back door.

"Put up your hood, Naddih. Cover your face. And wrap that tie before you trip on it. Man, not in a bow! Ninjas don't wear bows."

"Suhcrom, where's the ladder?"

"We don't have a ladder. We'll have to pile up some cinder blocks."

"But Jomfeh used a ladder the other day."

"That was Mr. Broomie's."

"Where is it?"

"He took it back—but I know where he put it."

Naddih gasped. "You were in Mr. Broomie's yard?"

"No man, no! I just watched from the fence."

"So if you know where it is, go get it."

"Man, mi no waa fi go ova deh. Dats askin' fi trouble."

"But you're a knight, remember?"

"All right, all right," Suhcrom sighed. "I'll get it."

His heart pounded as he climbed over the fence. He looked at Mr. Broomie's house. It was dark. His hands were moist with sweat and his legs wobbled as he jumped into the yard.

"Mi mus be crazy. Why mi listen to dat little boy." *Hiccup! Hiccup!*

"What was that noise?" asked Naddih.

"A bullfrog. Now shush!"

Cautiously, Suhcrom crept along the side of the fence, feeling his way in the dark. There it was, on the ground, right where his father had put it. *Ka-plunk, ka-plunk.* The ladder jostled as Suhcrom dragged it over the stones. *Ka-plunk, ka-plunk, ka-plunk.* He paused to glance one last time at the house... still no lights. He pushed the ladder up and over the fence where Naddih was waiting on the other side.

"Naddih, grab it."

"*Ouww*, my *ataritis!* This thing is too heavy!"

"Stop your belly-aching. Hurry up, before we get caught."

Naddih struggled to ease the ladder to the ground. Together, they carried it across their yard and leaned it securely against the house.

"To the roof, Suhcrom, to the roof!"

"Shhh, be quiet. Ninjas don't talk."

Naddih waved his sword and swiftly climbed the ladder. When he reached the roof, he walked around, fearlessly peering over the edge. He motioned to Suhcrom.

"Come on."

"I'm coming, I'm coming. Just hold on."

As he stepped on the first rung of the ladder, memories flashed through his mind of that horrible day months ago....

◖

... He'd been fidgety waiting for cartoons to come on. He couldn't sit still — not even for one minute. He'd been jittery, restless, and had no idea what to do.

"*Yu haunted,*" Enomih had said to him. "Why don't you clean up your room?"

He chuckled to himself as a strange expression

skipped through his mind—*go fly a kite, go fly a kite. Yeh, that's it.*

"I'm going to fly a kite!" he shouted.

"What's wrong with you, you crazy boy?"

"I'm going to go fly a kite!"

He gathered some coconut tree branches and pulled off the thread-like veins that ran down the center of the long blades. They were thin and pliable, yet strong enough to make a solid frame when tied together. He constructed the face of the kite with newspaper and flour paste. It wasn't fancy, but it worked. When it finished drying, he tied on a few strips of cloth from an old tee shirt and then attached a long nylon string. He couldn't wait to try it!

The best place to test it would have been the field by the Hart Academy, but he didn't feel like walking that far. So instead, he went to the roof. There was a strong breeze blowing that day and the kite instantly took flight. With every shift of the wind, he took a few steps forward and a few steps back. It wasn't long before he realized he was standing at the edge of the roof. He turned, but it was too late. Down he fell!

"*AAAAAAAAAAAH!*"

His arms flailed in the air. His body twisted and turned. He thought it was the end for him when his leg hit a concrete wash basin. He landed with a *THUD!* He lay on the ground, crumpled, dazed and confused. Twinkling stars swirled around in his head. He couldn't move, and he could barely breathe. In the distance, he could hear a voice calling out his name... a strangely familiar voice.

That's odd. My guardian angel sounds just like Mr. Broomie....

Since that day he had never climbed to the roof again—until now. His legs jiggled like jello as he stepped onto the ladder. His head was dizzy, but he kept on climbing. When he reached the top, he slowly eased himself off the ladder and onto the roof, and crawled away from the edge.

"*A weh yu a crawl pon yu belly fa, Suhcrom? Get up. Yu luk like Mista Slug.*"

Suhcrom took in a deep breath. "I'm lying low, checking for enemies."

"How are you going to run if you're on your belly? We're not going to crawl. We're going to run and jump from one house to the next. "

"*A wa mek yu so crazy, man!* I'm *NOT* doing this. I told you before, it's dangerous. We'll get killed!

"You promised."

"I'm having serious second, third *AND* fourth thoughts about this, Naddih." A sour taste gurgled up into his throat. He gulped and took another deep breath.

"You're a knight, Suhcrom. Knights aren't *fraidy-fraidy*. Knights are brave, remember?"

This was all Suhcrom needed to hear. He thought about the mission—about his book. He rose to his feet, determined to do whatever it would take to get his book back from Hamburg.

So together they ran, and jumped, from one roof top to the next. Naddih led the charge, sword in hand, feigning to slay the enemies along the way. It was a thrilling battle—until they landed on Hamburg's roof.

Grrrrrrr...grrrrrrrr.

"Oh no, it's Sticky."

"Suhcrom, let's slide down the drain pipe and go in Hamburg's bedroom window."

"The book isn't in his bedroom, Naddih. It's in the chicken coop."

"How do you know that?"

"I just know."

"What are we going to use to dress up Sticky?"

"We're here to get the book. Let's just get it and get out of here."

"But we were going to…."

"Shhh. Wait… I hear something." Suhcrom grabbed Naddih's arm just as he was about to slide down the drain pipe.

"It's Hamburg's mom… she'll see us. That lady has eyes in the back of her head!"

"This isn't going to work, Naddih. Let's get out of here."

Naddih charged back across the roof. Suhcrom trailed just steps behind. As they readied for the jump to their roof, Suhcrom heard some commotion on the street below. The distraction caused him to lose his focus. He stumbled as he jumped, barely catching the edge of the roof with his fingertips. He clung to the gutter. His legs dangled limply beneath him. One of his ninja stars slipped from his pocket, hitting against a stone below. *Klink!*

His head was spinning. Memories of their nomad adventure flashed through his mind, along with visions of the future — passing the Common Entrance Exam, going to high school, moving to America someday. There was so much he wanted to do. And there was still that unfulfilled promise to send money to Ethiopia.

"Are you going to come? Are you?" he called out.

"Suhcrom, I'm right here. Grab my hand."

"Where are you? Don't let me die. I promise I'll keep your secret. Come on, man, get on your magic broom and save me, Mista Brooooo…!"

"Who you talking to? I don't have no magic broom."

"Naddih, Naddih, please help me. Get me out of here, NOW!"

"Grab my hand… and hold on tight."

Naddih braced himself on his belly and locked hands with Suhcrom. He pulled and pulled with all of his might until Suhcrom was up on the roof.

"Get up. We need to get off the roof. Suhcrom, get up! They're going to see us."

Their hearts raced as they stepped onto solid ground.

"Leave the ladder. We'll take care of it later," said Suhcrom.

The neighbors were buzzing in conversation about the mysterious footsteps they had heard on the roofs. Suhcrom listened quietly to the chatter, but not Naddih. He darted right into the middle of the crowd, grinning from ear to ear, just itching to say something… and he did!

"Mi hear di footsteps dem too, yu know." His voice squeaked as he blurted out. "Sounded like people running… or a herd of bulls."

Suhcrom jabbed Naddih with his elbow. "Don't be

silly, man, a herd of bulls? Why don't you herd this." He grabbed Naddih by the ear, and before his brother could say another word, he dragged him into the house.

CHAPTER 7

The Run Home

I t was their first day back at Independence City All-Age School and the day couldn't end soon enough for Suhcrom. The very second the clock struck four-thirty he bolted out of his classroom to meet Naddih.

"You'll never believe this... one of our ninja stars!"

"Our ninja stars? What are you talking about?"

"Look." Suhcrom pulled the star out of his pocket. "It's a sign."

"A sign for what?"

"To finish our mission... tonight! We've got to get that book back."

"Yeh, and let's do battle with that Sticky!"

"We better hurry. We have lots to do. Come on, let's run."

"Run? How 'bout we take a taxi?"

"With what money? Don't be so silly."

"But I had P.E. today, Suhcrom. Miss Three-Level made us do like fifty million laps around the soccer field. My feet hurt!"

"We'll take the shortcut through the market like we've done before. It'll be fun. We'll be home in no time. Come on, let's do it."

"Oh, now I get it." Naddih crossed his arms and nodded. "You want to get home in time to watch cartoons."

Suhcrom grinned and gave Naddih a nudge with his elbow as he began to run. Naddih took a deep breath, flung his book bag over his shoulder and ran after him.

"Naddih, I want to be the baddest ninja ever!"

"I want to be the baddest ninja, too!"

"You can't be the baddest ninja 'cuz I'm already the baddest. You can be the second baddest. Let's go. If we hurry, we can be home in time for *He-Man!*"

"Slow down, Suhcrom. I can't keep up with you." Naddih doubled over, holding his stomach, trying to catch his breath. "My bag is too heavy."

"What do you have in that thing? It looks kind of puffy."

"Just my books and a few school supplies, like a notebook and pens and stuff."

Suhcrom opened the bag. He couldn't believe his eyes. It was like peering into Santa's Christmas sack! There were math and history books, a couple of puzzle books, five notebooks, a Bible, an encyclopedia....

"Wait a minute, what's this encyclopedia still doing in your book bag? Didn't I tell you to return this to the Waterford Public Library?"

Naddih shrugged his shoulders and stared at his brother. "I keep forgetting."

"For over a year?"

Naddih chuckled. "Remember Miss Rhondelle? She almost flunked me. Ten points she took off my grade — ten points for destroying public property, she said. I just wanted some nice pictures of the *hunch back* whales for my project."

"It's humpback whales, not *hunch back*."

Suhcrom held up the Bible. He raised his eyebrows and waived it in the air.

"I don't mean to sound unholy, but why are you carrying this in your book bag?"

"I carry it every day, Suhcrom, just like the preacher told us, remember? He said, 'Read it every day and use it as your guide.'"

"I remember exactly what he said, because he was lookin' straight at me when he said it!"

He rummaged through the rest of the bag. In addition to all of the books, he counted twelve pencils, ten pens, two pencil sharpeners and five erasers, three boxes of crayons, a silver compass and a rather nice wooden ruler … and a pair of dirty socks. He waved his hand in front of his nose and quickly tossed them aside.

"*Now mi see why yu so tired, man!* Why do you have all the back-to-school supplies in your bag? You know Jomfeh got them for all three of us, right?"

"But the heavier my bag is, the smarter I look to the rest of the kids."

"You don't need all of these things. You're only in third grade. All you need is a notebook and a couple of pencils. The encyclopedia belongs back at the library. And leave the puzzle books at home." Suhcrom took the encyclopedia, the Bible, the math and history books and put them in his bag. "There, now you don't have so much to carry. Let's get going. We're wasting time."

Side by side, the boys ran. They made it across the road and several blocks down the street. Then they paused to catch their breath.

"One … two … three … four … five. Go!"

"Wait, Suhcrom, wait," Naddih begged. "I need more air in my nostril. *Mi need fi rest a little bit longa.*"

"Wait? No way, man. We only have fifteen minutes before cartoons start."

Suhcrom dashed ahead of Naddih. They continued to run until they reached the middle of town. The streets buzzed with traffic. As they passed the first landmark, an almond tree, Suhcrom knew they were nearly half-way home. They would need to hustle to make it by five o'clock.

"The market is just ahead," he hollered.

Vendors lined the streets with their carts full of all kinds of fruits and vegetables. There were mangos, cherries, June plums, and tomatoes. There was cooked food, too. Some of the vendors recognized the boys.

"Howdy you two," they called out. "Grab a couple of mangos!"

"No thanks, not today... cartoons, cartoons," shouted Suhcrom. He waived as they raced past the carts.

The vendors chuckled and shook their heads. *"Man, luk at dem crazy boys. A weh dem a run so fast fa?"*

Suhcrom and Naddih passed the jerk pit. The savory smell of jerk chicken and pork filled the air, and it made their mouths water. Mr. Lindo's was the best. Nobody cooked jerk chicken the way he did—nobody! If there had been time, Suhcrom would have stopped to buy some. But he couldn't today. Today he and Naddih were on a mission. They stopped, took in one last deep breath of the sweet aroma—"Ahhhhhhh"—then surged ahead towards the gully.

The boys kept a fast, steady pace as they cut through

an open soccer field. Just before nearing the gully, Suhcrom stopped to catch his breath.

"One … two … three … four … five!" he shouted. He took off running again.

"Wait, Suhcrom. I'm going to fall to the ground. *Eeeeeh, eeeeeh.*"

"Okay, I'll give you five more seconds, but we don't have much time. Once we cross the gully we will almost be home."

"I can't cross the gully. I'm too tired."

"Don't worry, you can do it. Give me your book bag. Quick, hand it to me." Suhcrom grabbed both of their book bags and tossed them to the other side of the gully.

"What are you doing? Why did you throw my bag like that? It's going to be all dirty."

"Then just dust it off. It's going to be a whole lot easier to jump without it."

"Whoa, who said anything about jumping? I can't jump that thing today. I'll fall."

Naddih peered into the crevice of the gully. It was full of rocks, garbage and broken glass—and it stunk! "I'm not so sure I want to do this." He stared at the smelly pile of rubbish as Suhcrom jumped across the gully.

"Come on, Naddih. If you can run and jump across rooftops, you can jump this gully."

Naddih took a deep breath and plugged his nose. He lowered himself slowly into the gully until he reached a place where he felt safe to jump across, and then scooted up the other side of the embankment.

Suhcrom patted him on the back. "See, I knew you could do it."

They dusted themselves off, grabbed their book bags and crossed the intersection that led to Palmerston Close. Home was just around the corner.

"Last one there's a rotten-bellied pig," Suhcrom yelled.

With a sudden burst of renewed energy, Naddih took the lead.

"Oh no you don't," shouted Suhcrom. "No way I'm gonna let you beat me after all this!"

And so the boys ran, as fast as lightning, competing head to head toward the finish line. Suhcrom pulled ahead of Naddih by millimeters when they sprinted into the yard. They laughed and shoved each other as they stumbled into the house at exactly five o'clock. Suhcrom turned on the TV and flopped on the couch. *Phlumph!*

"*He-Man and the Masters of the Universe!*" they shouted.

CHAPTER 8

House Rules

L ater that evening, after supper, Suhcrom and Naddih huddled in front of the TV to secretly plan the completion of their mission. Naddih grabbed his notebook and pencil.

"Suhcrom, what is our *stratification?*"

"*Stratification?* I'm not even sure that's a word. And I don't know why you're writing this all down. I already have it written. Look."

"Well, what if you lose it? Then what would we do?"

"I have it all in here." Suhcrom pointed to his head and grinned.

"And we'll have my notes as a back-up."

"Okay, if you say so."

"So our mission is to go to Hamburg's and get the book?"

"That's right."

"And what book is it again?"

"The blue book with the white letters that say, 'New First Aid in English.' I need it to pass my Common

Entrance Exam. And you need it if you're ever going to beat Enomih at spelling!"

"Yes, she thinks she is so much smarter than us. Now, the part that's going to be a little tricky is dressing that yappy-mouthed dog!"

"The mission is to get my book, remember? Book first, dress Sticky second. Besides, that yappy-mouthed dog likes you. That part will be easy."

"Suhcrom, just imagine the look on Hamburg's face when he sees his favorite soccer jersey and shorts on his stinky-mouthed dog. Holy Moly, it will be so *FUNNY!*"

They roared with laughter at the thought. Suddenly, there was a knock at the front door.

"Who is it?" Naddih asked.

"It's me, Mikal, open up."

"Quick, Naddih, hide our plans."

Suhcrom shoved his paper under the couch cushion. Naddih panicked. He ripped the piece of paper from his notebook, wadded it up and stuffed it in his mouth. His eyes watered. They grew bigger and bigger as he chewed and chewed and chewed. When he began to gag and choke, he spit the paper out into his hand and stuffed it under the cushion along with Suhcrom's notes.

"What did you do that for? That's disgusting."

"Guys, can I come in?" Mikal shouted.

The boys laughed and called out together, "Come on in, big dummy!"

Mikal opened the door just as the theme song to *Sanford and Son* started playing. *Doodup doodup… doodup doodup doodup doo… doodup doodup….*

"Who's the big dummy, dummies?" Mikal joked.

"*Yu di big dummy,*" said Suhcrom.

"No, yu di big dummy," Mikal said, shoving Suhcrom's arm.

"No, yu di big dummy," Naddih chuckled.

"Oh, guys wait, wait. Everybody in Palmerston Close heard about your new color TV. So Amos, Sterlin, Rodney and Hamburg are on their way over. They can't wait to see it!"

No sooner had Mikal made his announcement when another knock came at the door.

Naddih giggled mischievously. "*WhoIZZit?*"

"It's Amos, Sterlin, Rodney and Hamburg."

The four boys waited and waited. They heard *Sanford and Son* playing on the TV, and they didn't want to miss any of it. But no one had yet given permission for them to come in.

Bam! Bam! Bam! "Come on guys, open up! We're missing the show!"

Naddih, Suhcrom and Mikal all yelled together as Naddih opened the door, "Come on in big dummies."

"Who's the big dummies?" asked Amos as he bounded through the door.

"*Alla yu a big dummies,*" Naddih laughed.

"Mr. 'ford's on, huh?" Hamburg said excitedly.

"Yes," said Mikal, "And we get to watch him on this brand new color TV. I've never seen anything like this in my life!"

"Wow, how did they do this? It looks so real," said Hamburg.

"I bet you don't miss that old clunky black and white," Sterlin chuckled. "That thing was a piece of junk."

"I know we won't be missing it, isn't that right guys?" said Amos.

"Yeh," agreed Hamburg. "Naddih, I bet you're happy you don't have to hold the antenna anymore!"

These comrades loved watching *Sanford and Son* together, and there was nothing better than watching it in color. They all chimed in as the theme song played again. "*Doodup doodup … doodup doodup doodup doo … doodup doodup ….*" At the next commercial, Naddih stood up in front of the TV to make an important announcement.

"Okay, guys, here are the house rules."

"Oh man, not house rules again. Naddih, you tell them to us every time we come over here," Sterlin grumbled.

Amos, Mikal and Hamburg all moaned. "I think we know them all by now."

"Yeh, but don't somebody always break them?" asked Rodney.

"So, let's go over them."

"Whatever you say, man, whatever," Mikal groaned. He shoved Amos with his foot. "Move over."

"Hurry up, Naddih, Mr. 'ford's coming back on, like in seconds," Sterlin said.

"Okay, okay. Now you guys can use the bathroom. It's over there on the left, understood?" Naddih paused and waited for them to nod.

"Yeh, yeh, we got it," they all chimed.

"Okay, and you can eat whatever is in the fridge, but do not, and I repeat, do NOT eat the food left on the stove. That is for me and Suhcrom. Got it?"

"Yes, we got it already," Mikal complained. "Come on, finish up, man."

"Okay, now don't go into any of the bedrooms, especially Jomfeh's. His is strictly off-limits. And finally, the most important thing of all, don't fall asleep in this house unless you live here. If you fall asleep, *dog eat yu suppa. Unu get weh mi a seh?*"

"Yes, yes, Naddih we understand! Now get out of the way," they all shouted. "Mr. *'ford* is on, man."

The boys were glued to the screen for the rest of the show, and when it ended, Suhcrom turned the TV off. It was in that moment that they all heard it—the strangely familiar sound.

"Zzzzzzzzz ... *snort-snort.*"

"Amos is snoring! Guys, look, Amos is in dreamland," Mikal chuckled.

Their heads turned in unison to stare at their sleeping comrade. He was slouched on the floor with his back against the chair, sound asleep with his mouth wide open. Naddih stared in disbelief.

"Amos is breaking the house rules."

"Oh man, are we going to have fun with this," Mikal laughed. "Hey 'Burg, hit that light behind you."

Hamburg flipped off the lights. As soon as the room went dark, they each grabbed a cushion. *Whack! Thump! Pip! Bop! Conk!* Amos stirred at the first strike, screaming and squirming with every blow.

"Ahhh, oooh, I'll get you for this!"

He kicked his legs and tried to crawl away, wildly swinging his arms. With Amos out of the middle, the boys turned on themselves. It was an all-out brawl. Their laughter grew louder and louder—and they were

having the time of their lives!

Naddih rushed to protect the TV. "Guys, guys, don't knock the TV. Have some mercy here!"

"Yeh, guys, take this outside," said Suhcrom. "If we break it, we'll all be in big trouble. And I don't want to go back to eatin' sardine for six months to save for another one."

"You're right, you're right," Mikal agreed. "Last one out kisses Sticky Fingers... on the mouth!"

"Yuck, that's gross," Sterlin moaned. "Nobody wants to kiss stinky-mouth Sticky Fingers. Do you know where that dog's mouth has been?"

"Oh no! I don't want to kiss Sticky Fingers," Rodney screeched. "That's yucky!"

Suddenly it was a madhouse as they all raced toward the front door. It was a battle to see who would get out first. Mikal, who was the oldest, was an expert runner from playing soccer. He was fast. No one could come close to matching his speed. He darted out the door, leaving everyone else behind in a heap.

Hamburg tugged at Sterlin's arm, trying to hold him back. Young Rodney got knocked to the floor. He grabbed Hamburg's leg and held on with all his might.

"I don't want to be last!"

Amos, still struggling to get his bearings, got lost

in the shuffle. Sterlin lunged forward. He jerked loose of Hamburg's grip and flew out the door. Hamburg, attempting to break away from Rodney's grip, dragged him across the floor. He finally got loose and fled, on Sterlin's heels.

Rodney ended up with brush burns on his belly. As soon as Hamburg had bolted, he popped up off the floor and ran out the door right behind him. That left Amos for last. No sooner had he stepped out the door when all the boys were on him like flies, tumbling and tossing each other about the yard.

"Amos has to kiss Sticky Fingers! Ha-ha-ha! Amos has to kiss stinky-mouth Sticky Fingers!" they all teased.

Suhcrom watched the chaos with amusement. "Those guys are crazy, man. We better clean this place up before Enomih gets home or we'll be in BIG trouble. You know how she is when she's in charge."

"Yeh, she thinks she is the boss of us. She punishes us worse than Jomfeh."

Suhcrom grabbed a cushion and tossed it on the couch. "Holy Moly, Naddih, look what I found... our notes! Good thing those guys didn't see them."

CHAPTER 9

The Final Mission

By the time the boys got the living room back in order, their friends had long since gone home.

"Suhcrom, we're doing the mission tonight, right?"

"Yes, definitely. It's time."

"Those guys will *NEVER* guess we're *ninja-ing* around in their back yards."

"*Ninja-ing*? What kind of word is that?"

"That's what I call it when ninjas are sneaking around at night."

"Oh, I see," laughed Suhcrom.

"Let me see your notes. Mine are too soggy."

Naddih chuckled at the wad of mushy paper in his hands. He took another look at Suhcrom's notes and scratched his head, carefully reviewing every detail of the mission.

"Okay, first we cross Mikal's yard, then climb into Hamburg's, get the book, dress Sticky...."

"*Man, a weh yu keep repeatin' di wul plan fa?*"

"I just want to make sure I get it right, that's all."

"Remember, book first. That's the important thing. I need that book."

"What about dressing Sticky?"

"Only if there's time. But it would be a funny trick on Hamburg.

"Yah mon, so funny!"

"Let's get our ninja clothes on, Naddih. Where did you put Jomfeh's old ties?"

"The ones with the curry stains?"

"Yea, yea, Jomfeh and his curry shrimp! Where are they? And which shirt do you want, black or dark, dark, dark blue? Keep in mind, I want the black one."

"A weh yu ask mi fa den if mi no have a choice?"

"It doesn't really matter. Besides, we're wearing them at night. Who's going to be able to tell the difference?"

"Give mi di black one den."

Suhcrom slipped on his pants and shirt, flipped his hood over his head and wrapped the tie around his waist. He glanced in the mirror and winked at himself.

"Mirror, mirror, lookin' my way. Who's the baddest ninja today?"

Naddih jumped into his pants and threw on his shirt. It twisted and puckered as he wound the tie around his waist. He wrapped it around and around, and around one more time, pulled it as tight as he could, and tied it in a huge knot.

"Move over, move over, let me get some mirror time."

"Okay, Mista Handsome Chap. But don't spend too much time lookin' at yourself. Meet me at the location."

"Where are our stars and swords? We can't forget them."

He slipped a star into his pocket, grabbed his sword and ran to catch up with his brother. He was halfway out the front door when he heard a loud shout.

"Naddih, NADDIH! The back door, man. We're going out the back door."

"Oh, mi forget."

"Holy Moly, did you really look at yourself?"

"Why, what's so funny?"

"Your ninja belt... can you breath?"

"Nuttin' wrong wid it."

"This is going to be a fun night for a mission! We better get out of here before Enomih sees us." He pulled Naddih by the arm and darted out the back door.

"You remember the plan, right?"

"Yes, yes, I remember it.

"You should. You went over it like a million times!"

"Cross Mikal's yard into Hamburg's, get the book. Dress Sticky Fingers... if there's time," Naddih recited.

"Okay, let's go. No talking."

"Okay."

"Silence starting now." Suhcrom motioned to zip their lips.

The coconut tree branches swayed back and forth in the heavy breeze as the boys crossed their yard to the fence that bordered Mikal's. A soft stream of light filtered between the houses from the street lamp out front. They could hear some faint chatter from the neighbors visiting in the street. They paused when they reached the fence.

"Let go of me, man."

"I thought you said no talking."

"How can I be quiet when you're clutchin' my shirt so tight and squeezin' my hand? You're cutting off my circulation."

Naddih released his hold and they pulled themselves up to peer over the fence into Mikal's yard.

"It's clear," Suhcrom whispered.

They jumped in tandem, landing without a sound, and started across Mikal's yard. Suhcrom's heart pounded with anticipation. Finally he would have his book back. He silently pledged to read and study more from now on... knowing there was nothing that would make his father more proud than to see him pass his Common Entrance Exam.

All of a sudden, Suhcrom stopped dead in his tracks. He held his arm out to stop Naddih. "Shhh."

"What is it?"

"Someone's coming!"

They dashed to the back of Mikal's yard where it was pitch black. They crouched down, in the darkness, waiting silently... and barely breathing.

"It's Mikal. He's talking to someone."

"Who's he talking to? What's he saying?"

"Shhh... I can't hear... I think he's talking to Hamburg."

"About what?"

"Man, if you let me listen, then we will know. Shhh."

They waited... and waited... and waited. Finally they heard Mikal say, "Okay, man, see you tomorrow." They heard a door open, and then slam shut. *Bang!*

"Man, that boy is always slammin' doors," said Naddih. "Do you remember when he...?"

"Dang, I missed the entire conversation. Can't you be quiet for two seconds? You and that mouth will get in a whole heap of trouble one day."

Suhcrom looked at the house. He motioned to Naddih that the coast was clear once again. They crept over to the fence that bordered Hamburg's yard.

Adrenaline rushed through their veins just thinking

about their near discovery the last time they were here. This time the mission was going to be a little trickier. Suhcrom ran every detail through his mind. He didn't want to mess this up! He needed to get into the chicken coop, find his book, and get out fast!

"Keep Sticky away from me. I mean it, man. Keep that dog away from me while I search the coop."

"What makes you think the book is in the coop?"

"I just know ... that's all."

Naddih snuck up to the fence. "Suhcrom, lift me up so I can see if Sticky is there." He clung to the cinderblocks while Suhcrom hoisted him onto his shoulders. He peaked into Hamburg's yard. Startled, he quickly pulled back.

"Abort mission," he gasped. "Abort!"

Suhcrom dropped Naddih to the ground and clasped his hand over his mouth. "One more word and I'll ... "

"No man, it's Hamburg. He's still outside."

"Let me see. Yah mon, you're right. He's sitting on that rickety wooden chair, holding a flashlight ... and he's reading a book—to Sticky. He's got the book!"

"Reading to Sticky? Suhcrom, that boy is crazy, you know. Why would he be reading a book to a dog?"

"I don't know. Why do you talk to your pigeons? Now be quiet. He's going to hear us."

A noise caught their attention. Hamburg's mom leaned out the door and called him in for supper. "I'm coming," he answered. He tossed the book and flashlight on the chair and skipped into the house.

Suhcrom looked at Naddih; their eyes grew wide like saucers. "Go!" said Suhcrom. Without another word, they leaped over the fence. Suhcrom had the book in his sight as he raced toward the chair.

"Oh, mi big toe," he yelped. He stumbled and fell into the chair, knocking it over. The book sailed across the yard out of his reach.

ARRRF-ARRRF! ARRRF-ARRRF-ARRRF!

"Shush, good doggy, good doggy," Naddih said, patting Sticky Fingers on the head. He glanced at the clothesline. "Suhcrom, where's Hamburg's jersey and soccer shorts? I gotta dress Sticky."

"No time. We need to leave ... NOW. We're going to get caught! And I'm not sticking around to get bitten by a stinky-mouth dog!" Suhcrom made a mad dash and scaled the fence into Mikal's yard. He never looked back.

Suddenly, he heard voices. It was Naddih and Hamburg's mom. Panic set in. Suhcrom knew he couldn't save Naddih, not now. But he could still save himself. So he hightailed to their house, raced to his bedroom and

shut the door. He stripped off his ninja outfit and put on his pajamas.

Meanwhile, Naddih was left to fend for himself with Hamburg's mother. She pulled down his hood. Sticky Fingers stood guard, growling under his breath, ready to pounce if Naddih made a wrong move.

"What are you doing sneaking around in my back yard at this time of the night, Naddih Nadhallom? *Mi a go tell yu faada!*" She grabbed Naddih by the ear and pulled him into the house. "*A weh yuh dress like dis fa?*"

"Let me explain, Miss Hamburg's mom. Give me a second... *ouch* ... I was pretending to be a ninja...."

"Why don't you pretend to be a ninja when you get a whoopin' from your father."

"Please Miss Hamburg's mom. Please, let me go home. Can't we let bygones be bygones? I won't do it again. I promise. I'll just jump back over the fence and go home."

"No! Absolutely not Mister Ninja Man."

With a firm hold on his left ear, she led Naddih into her house, through the kitchen and past the living room. Hamburg was watching TV and heard the commotion. He glanced up just as his mother dragged Naddih past the doorway. Naddih raised his hand in a limp wave.

"Where are you taking me?"

"You have some more explaining to do!"

She dragged him out the front door in view of all the neighbors. Some of the grown-ups were sitting around, playing dominoes, and a group of kids were playing cricket under the street lamps. They all stopped to stare at Hamburg's mother.

"Woman, whose ear are you pulling on this time?" Everyone gasped when they realized it was Naddih.

"He was sneaking around in my back yard. Got my dog yappin so loud... scared me half out of my wits!"

"I can explain...."

"Shush, you can save your explaining for when your father comes home. Now go."

Naddih hung his head as he walked back to his house, knowing that he had gotten off easy. So many thoughts went through his mind. The secret ninja mission was blown, and to top it off, Suhcrom had left him behind to take the blame. There would be another price to pay when his father learned of this, and there would be no more secret missions ever again.

"Suhcrom," he called out as he walked into his house. "Suhcrom?" There was no response. He shuffled into the bedroom, closed the door and hopped into bed. Thoughts raced through his mind. He tossed and turned and thought about Hamburg's mother and how she scolded him in front of the whole neighborhood.

"How can a grown-up do that to a child? And how could my own brother leave me alone like that?"

He grabbed his covers and stared at the wall as he laid his head on the pillow. Something on the wall caught his eye. It was faded, yet still visible.

"Hmm, that's weird," he said to himself. "What is that?" Naddih tipped his head and looked more closely. "I remember that. I drew that when I was a little kid."

His head flooded again with memories of all the great adventures he and Suhcrom had taken. They'd had so much fun. No one could ever take that excitement away! He didn't want it to end… not like this. He jumped out of bed, flung open the door and raced out to the living room. He saw Suhcrom sitting on the couch scribbling on a piece of paper. Suhcrom cast an apologetic look in Naddih's direction.

"I'm sorry about what happened earlier," he said softly.

"Mi know, mi know." Naddih smirked and threw a wink at his brother as he darted out the back door.

"Where are you going?"

"The mission!"

Minutes later, he burst back through the door, out of breath. "I did it! Ha-ha, I did it, Suhcrom!" He twirled around and around and jumped high into the air.

"What? What are you talking about? Tell me!"

"I dressed up Hamburg's dog! I dressed up Hamburg's dog!"

"What about the book? Did you get the book?"

"The book?"

"It was all about the book."

"Well, if you want your book, then why don't you act like a big man and just go over there and ask him for it? That's all you have to do. Just ask."

"Act like a big man? I'm grown up now. I AM a big man."

"Okay then, let's go."

"Go where, Naddih?"

"Over to Hamburg's. I'll go with you."

Naddih pulled his brother off the couch. He grabbed him by the hand, dragged him out the door and led him to Hamburg's house.

Knock-knock-knock! Knock-knock-knock! The door creaked open and Hamburg peaked outside.

"Who is it, Hamburg?" his mother shouted. She quickly came to the door. "What are you doing back here, little boy?"

"We are here for business not pleasure, Miss Hamburg's mom. We're both here to talk to him."

Suhcrom and Naddih pointed their fingers at Hamburg.

"What do you want to talk with him about?"

"Please Miss Hamburg's mom. It's very important. All we need is a few seconds."

"You kids..." she mumbled under her breath and walked away.

"So what is so important?" Hamburg asked.

"We know you have Suhcrom's book."

"What book?"

"The one you've been using to study spelling," Suhcrom said.

"Yeh, the one you were reading to the dog earlier. Suhcrom wants it back."

"I'm still using it."

"You've had it for a couple of weeks now. He needs it back. He has to study, too."

"All right, all right. Hold on, I'll get it."

Hamburg disappeared. The boys stood silently, waiting and wondering. The seconds seemed like minutes, the minutes like hours. Then they heard a voice call out.

"Come in here, little boy."

"Suhcrom, who's she talking to?"

"You're littler than me."

"Naddih, come in here."

Naddih tiptoed into the house. Halfway down the

hallway, he was met by Hamburg's mom. His legs trembled. His ear prickled with pain.

"Come over here," she said again, more softly this time. "I'm sorry I embarrassed you in front of the neighbors. You scared me half to death roaming around in my back yard. You know I just want you to be safe."

"Yes, ma'am."

"Here, take some ice cream. I have a nice chocolate fudgesicle for you. And a couple pieces of bubble gum."

"Thanks, Miss Hamburg's mom!" He stuffed a piece of bubble gum in his mouth and took a bite of the ice cream. When he returned to the front door, Suhcrom was waiting for him on the veranda, ready to go back home.

"Look, got my book."

"See how easy that was? And we did that whole ninja mission for nothin'."

"Man, I never thought Hamburg would give it up so easily. I can't believe we did all of that silly stuff. I nearly died falling off the roof!"

"And all you had to do is ask for it."

"I don't think he's seen his dog yet."

"Yah mon, Sticky looks so funny!"

"Where did you get that fudgesicle?"

"From Miss Hamburg's mom."

"Can I have a lick?"

"Here, you can have some bubble gum."

Suhcrom unwrapped the gum. He looked at the picture on the wrapper. "Hey Naddih, look at this...Superman."

"Wow, *THUPERman!*" Ice cream and bubble gum flew out of his mouth when he shouted. "Ha-ha, last one home is a rotten chicken egg!"

Suhcrom snickered and pushed his brother aside. The boys ran towards home, laughing and giggling, shoving each other playfully back and forth.

"Hey, Suhcrom, you'll never guess what I saw on the bedroom wall...!"

Patois Words and Phrases
(Presented in order of appearance by chapter)

Main Characters
Suhcrom – (SU crom)

Naddih – (NA dee)

Enomih – (ee NO mee)

Evrohl – (EV roll); also known as Jomfeh (JOM fay)

Chapter 1—Close Call
8 *A who de out deh? Mi seh, a who de outside deh? Mi a go come out deh and put a whoopin' pon yu if yu no show yu face!*—Who's out there? I said, who's outside there? I'm going to come out there and put a whipping on you if you don't show your face!

12 *When mi get bigga, mi a go show yu who is smaata.*—When I get bigger, I'm going to show you who is smarter.

12 Common Entrance exam—A crucial examination taken by students at the end of 6th grade. If passed it meant automatic promotion to Secondary School. Students make a list of schools they wish to attend, and based on the results of the examination, they

are placed at a school from their list. This test was discontinued in 1999 when it was replaced by the GSAT (Grade Six Achievement Test).

13 *Jus imagine when mi get dem bigga!*—Just imagine when they get bigger!

14 *Mi tink dem hav muscle inna dem eye lash, too.*—I think they have muscles in their eye lashes, too.

14 *gungo peas*—a small round bean, similar to a lentil; also called "pigeon peas"; used in traditional Jamaican foods like soups or stews, or eaten with rice.

Chapter 2—Annoying Rooster

18 *A weh yu deh outside inna yu underpants fa?*—What are you doing outside in your underpants?

22 *How wi a go do alla dat in one day?*—How are we going to do all of that in one day?

23 *Di paint cans betta because dem no break!*—The paint cans are better because they don't break!

23 *Wi need waata inna di cans.*—We need water in the cans.

24 *Mi did a preten fi be a pirate anna dig fi treasure!*—I pretended to be a pirate and I was digging for treasure!

25 *Mi need Mista Swazenaada to help mi wid dis.*—I

need Mister Swazenaada (Schwarzenegger) to help me with this.

25 *Mi like dat betta.* — I like that better.

25 *Mi na bawl, mi jus a speak mi mind.* — I'm not bawling, I'm just speaking my mind.

26 *Mi dun, man. Mi wi wok pon mi imboorance lataron* — I'm done, man. I will work on my *imboorance* later on.

Chapter 3 — Soccer Some Books

29 *A wah yuh boys a talk 'bout?* — What are you boys talking about?

31 *ska* — a kind of Jamaican music that blends several forms of music such as calypso and jazz; a precursor to reggae.

32 *Because di big toe wud mek di most noise.* — Because the big toe would make the most noise.

32 Mi so *blahdy tirsty.* — I'm so bloody thirsty. (imitating the British expression)

32 *Yah mon* — literally means, "Yes, man"; a very commonly used phrase in Jamaica, similar to saying, "Okay, man."

Chapter 4 — Ninja Stars

34 *How wi a go mek a star outta metal?* — How are we going to make a star out of metal?

34 *Mi stronga now!*—I'm stronger now!

35 *Mi know, mi know.*—I know, I know.

37 *Mi dun wid dis ting ya.*—I am finished with this thing.

39 *A weh yu do dat fa?*—What did you do that for?

42 *No, no, mi seh no, man.*—No, no, I said no, man.

42 *Every ting betta now. Every ting much betta.*—Everything's better now. Everything's much better.

Chapter 5—Pop Quiz

47 *Mi dun wid studyin' for tonight.*—I'm done with studying for tonight.

49 *Mi no know 'bout dat.*—I don't know about that.

50 *Well, Jomfeh seh mi curious. Dats why mi ask so many questions.*—Well, Jomfeh says I'm curious. That's why I ask so many questions.

50 *Mi smaat, right?*—I'm smart, right?

Chapter 6—Desperate Measures

51 *So, a weh yu tink?*—So what do you think?

51 *Tell mi wa deh pon yu mind.*—Tell me what is on your mind.

52 *Mi no fraid no more. Mi wi slay Mista Daakness.*—I'm not afraid any more. I will slay Mister Darkness.

52 *fool-fool*—foolish

53 *Mi dun now.*—I'm done now.

53 *fraidy-fraidy*—afraid; or fraidy-cat

53 *Mi know, Suhcrom. Mi a go kill alla di enemies wid mi sword.*—I know, Suhcrom. I'm going to kill all of the enemies with my sword.

54 *Man, mi no waa fi go ova deh. Dats askin' fi trouble.*—Man, I don't want to go over there. That's asking for trouble.

54 *Mi mus be crazy. Why mi listen to dat little boy.*—I must be crazy. Why did I listen to that little boy.

55 *Yu haunted*—You're restless; fidgety; agitated

57 *A weh yu a crawl pon yu belly fa, Suhcrom? Get up. Yu luk like Mista Slug.*—What are you crawling on your stomach for, Suhcrom? Get up. You look like Mister Slug.

57 *A wa mek yu so crazy, man!*—What makes you so crazy, man!

61 *Mi hear di footsteps dem too, yu know.*— I heard those footsteps too, you know.

Chapter 7—The Run Home

66 *Now mi see why yu so tired, man.*—Now I see why you are so tired, man.

66 *Mi need fi rest a little bit longa.*—I need to rest a little bit longer.

67 *Man, luk at dem crazy boys. A weh dem a run so fast fa?* — Man, look at those carzy boys. What are they running so fast for?

Chapter 8 — House Rules

73 *Yu di big dummy.* — You're the big dummy.

74 *Alla yu a big dummies.* — All of you are big dummies.

75 *dog eat yu suppa* — A Jamaican proverb that is a warning that you will be punished / something bad will happen to you.

75 *Unu get weh mi a seh ?* — Do you get what I'm saying?

Chapter 9 — The Final Mission

81 *Man, a weh yu keep repeatin' di wul plan fa?* — Man, why do you keep repeating the whole plan?

82 *A weh yu ask mi fa den if mi no have a choice?* — What did you ask me for if I don't have a choice?

82 *Give mi di black one den.* — Give me the black one then.

83 *Oh, mi forget.* — Oh, I forgot.

83 *Nuttin' wrong wid it.* — Nothing wrong with it.

89 *Mi a go tell yu faada!* — I'm going to tell your father!

89 *A weh yuh dress like dis fa?* — What are you dressed like that for?

91 *Mi know, mi know.* — I know, I know.

About the Authors

Marcus E. Mohalland was born in Jamaica and was raised in communities that, according to Jamaican standards, were in between poor and middle class. Many of his own life experiences are recounted in this story. He obtained his Master's degree from Binghamton University and resides in Vestal, N.Y. "I have always desired to write about my life in a way that would encourage youth to enjoy their childhood, be grateful for what they have, and motivate them to achieve their greatest potential."

Janet L. Lewis Zelesnikar was born and raised in Endicott, New York. She obtained her Bachelor's degree from Syracuse University and is a Registered Nurse. She lives in Endwell, N.Y. with her husband, John, and her best furry friend, Sam. "Every child deserves to have fun as they grow and learn and should be encouraged to use their imagination. I was privileged to have such a childhood."

Visit our website at www.mohallandlewisllc.com to learn more about us and our company. Also find us on Facebook—Search Silly Nomads.

SILLY NOMADS SERIES

Vol. 1 Silly Nomads From Palmerston Close

Vol. 2 Silly Nomads Go Ninja Crazy

STAY TUNED...

THERE'S MORE SILLY NOMADS

COMING SOON...

Vol 3 Silly Nomads Make Great Superheroes

"WI SO SILLY, MAN!"